# MY FIRST
# PICTURE BOOK
## ABOUT
# JESUS

Bethan James and
Nadine Wickenden

CONCORDIA PUBLISHING HOUSE · SAINT LOUIS

Mary put baby Jesus in a manger.
There was no room for them in the inn.

Point to the baby in the manger.

Shepherds ran to Bethlehem to find
the special baby. Angels told them where to find Him.

How many sheep can you see?

Wise Men from the East followed a star to the baby King.
They gave Jesus gifts of gold, frankincense, and myrrh.

How did the Wise Men travel?

Jesus was baptized when He was a man.
John baptized Him in the River Jordan.

Can you see the dove?

Jesus lived by Lake Galilee.
He asked some fishermen to be His disciples.

How many boats are on the lake?

The wine ran out at a wedding in Cana.
Jesus changed jars of water into wonderful wine.

How many jars are there?

Jesus healed a man who couldn't walk.
His friends lowered him through a hole in the roof!

Count the man's friends.

Jesus told people not to worry.
God would give them everything they needed.

God gave us what we need most: a Savior from sin.

What color are the flowers in the field?

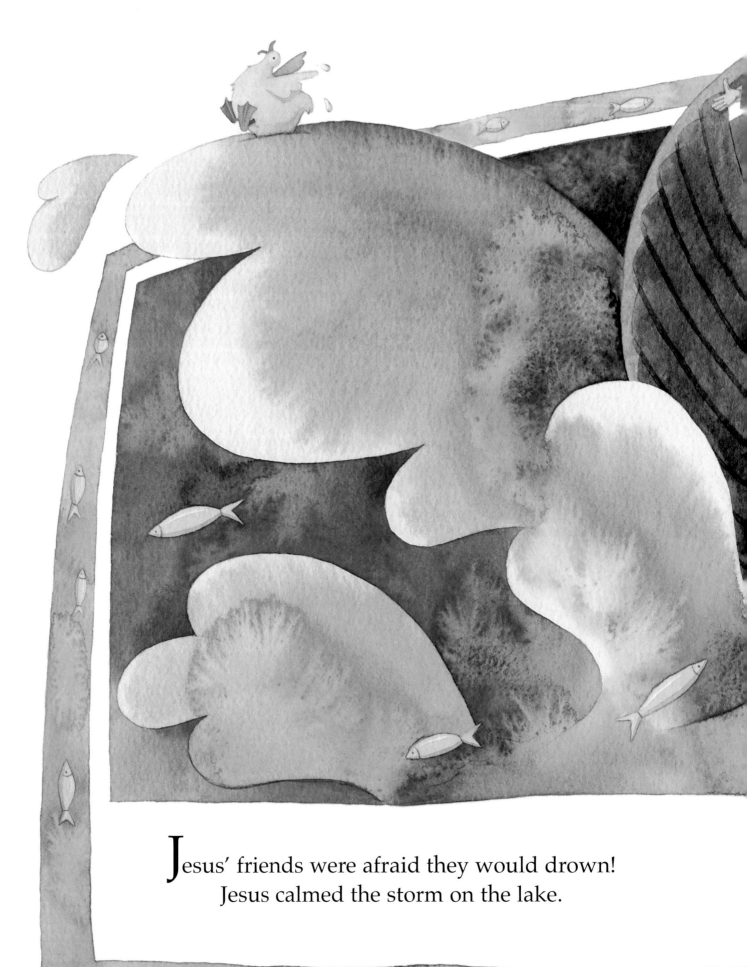

Jesus' friends were afraid they would drown!
Jesus calmed the storm on the lake.

Jesus is God the Son.

Count the men in the boat.

Jesus cared about people who were old.
He healed a woman who had been ill for a long time.

Touch the edge of Jesus' cloak.

Jesus cared about people who were young.
He made Jairus's daughter well after she had died.

See how happy her parents are!

A boy once shared his lunch with Jesus.
Jesus changed the small lunch into a big meal for everyone!

Can you see the boy
with five loaves and two fish?

Jesus helped anyone who came to Him.
He told us to be kind to everyone we see.

Find the two men who
didn't stop to help.

Jesus told us that God loves us very much.
God loves us like the shepherd looking for his lost sheep.

Look at the wolf's sharp teeth!

Bartimaeus called out to Jesus to help him.
Jesus helped the blind man to see.

Bartimaeus jumped for joy.

Jesus talked to people who had no friends.
Zacchaeus had climbed a tree to see Him!

Can you see the figs on the branches?

Jesus rode into Jerusalem on a donkey.
People shouted, "Here is Jesus, the King!"

Count the palm branches on the ground.

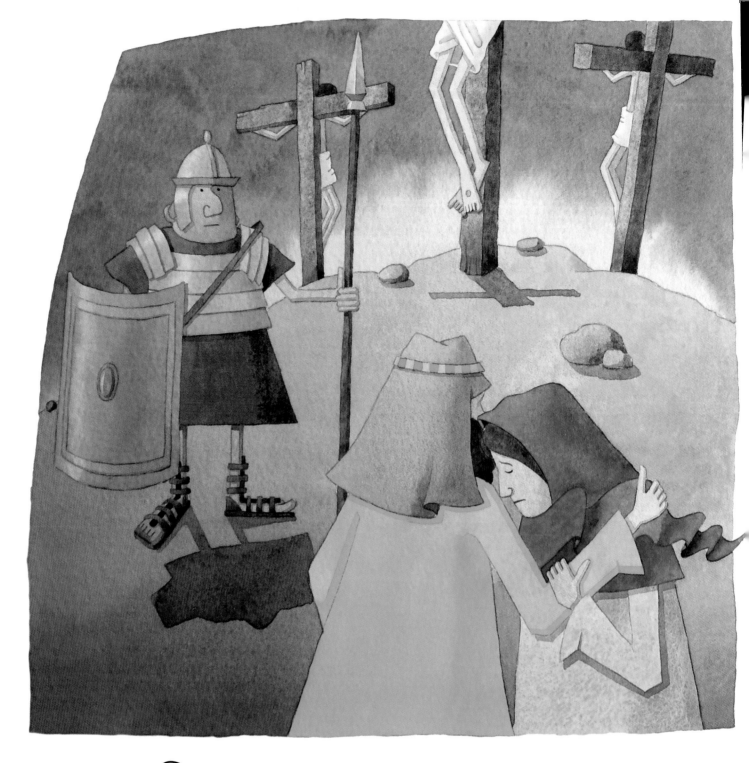

Some people didn't like what Jesus was doing
and had Him killed.
His friends were very sad.

Can you see His mother crying?

Jesus was buried in a tomb, but God raised Him from the grave.
Mary spoke to Him in the garden.

Point to the stone that has been rolled away.

Jesus was alive again.
All His friends saw Him.
Jesus even had breakfast with the disciples
one morning.

Look at the fish Jesus helped them catch.

This edition published by Concordia Publishing House
3558 S. Jefferson Ave., St. Louis, MO 63118-3968
1-800-325-3040 • www.cph.org
ISBN 978-0-7586-1330-1

First edition 2007

Copyright © 2007 Anno Domini Publishing
1 Churchgates, The Wilderness, Berkhamsted, Herts HP4 2UB England
Text copyright © 2007 Bethan James
Illustrations copyright © 2007 Nadine Wickenden

Editorial Director Annette Reynolds
Editor Nicola Bull
Art Director Gerald Rogers
Pre-production Krystyna Kowalska Hewitt
Production John Laister

Printed and bound in Singapore